PAPPY'S HANDKERCHIEF

BY *Devin Scillian*

ILLUSTRATED BY *Chris Ellison*

—◆◇◆—

SLEEPING BEAR PRESS
TALES *of* YOUNG AMERICANS SERIES

For my wife, sounding board, collaborator, and best friend Corey.
May the spirit of Oklahoma stay with us forever.

DEVIN

To the families who generously gave of their time for this project.

CHRIS

Text Copyright © 2007 Devin Scillian
Illustration Copyright © 2007 Chris Ellison

Sleeping Bear Press™

310 North Main Street, Suite 300
Chelsea, MI 48118
www.sleepingbearpress.com

©2007 Sleeping Bear Press is an imprint of The Gale Group, Inc.

Printed and bound in China.

10 9 8 7 6 5 4 3 2 1

ISBN: 978-1-58536-316-2
Library of Congress publication data on file.

March 25, 1889 - Baltimore, Maryland

The icy air smelled like salt and as the fishermen laid out the bounty of their nets, large snowflakes began to land on the dark green waves off the Baltimore pier. As I did every day, I ran from home at lunchtime to help my father in our fish stall. But with the weather getting worse and a meager day's catch from the fishermen, there were few takers for the goods on my father's table. Still, I cried out to the passersby as always.

"Codfish! Bluefish! Fresh today!

Clams and oysters fresh from the bay!"

AUTHOR'S NOTE

The great Oklahoman Will Rogers once said, "You've got to go out on a limb sometimes because that's where the fruit is." Rogers' home state was founded by people who believed exactly that. In settling the Oklahoma Territory, they were out on a limb grasping for the fruit we've come to know as the American dream.

The day of April 22, 1889 began with an empty plain in Oklahoma. By nightfall, homesteads stretched to the horizon, and Oklahoma City and Guthrie had suddenly sprung to life, each with an instant population of 10,000 people.

The history of Oklahoma is terribly complicated. Opening up the Oklahoma Territory for settlers meant, of course, taking the land away from Native Americans who endured unspeakable hardships. At the same time, it allowed others the chance at a new life. That included many African Americans, like the family in this story. When President Benjamin Harrison announced the first Land Run in 1889, word began to spread among black Americans, some believing that if enough African Americans made the westward journey to stake a claim, Oklahoma could become an all black state. For a variety of reasons, that didn't happen. But the Land Runs created a unique opportunity for many African American families, and, at one time, Oklahoma had more all black towns than any other state.

While we talk about *the* Oklahoma Land Run, there were actually five different runs between 1889 and 1895. *Pappy's Handkerchief* isn't about any one family or even one land run. The story is a medley of the struggles and experiences of thousands of families who journeyed west to live as pioneers on the prairie. They were way out on a limb, and the fruit they harvested is alive in the spirit of Oklahoma today.

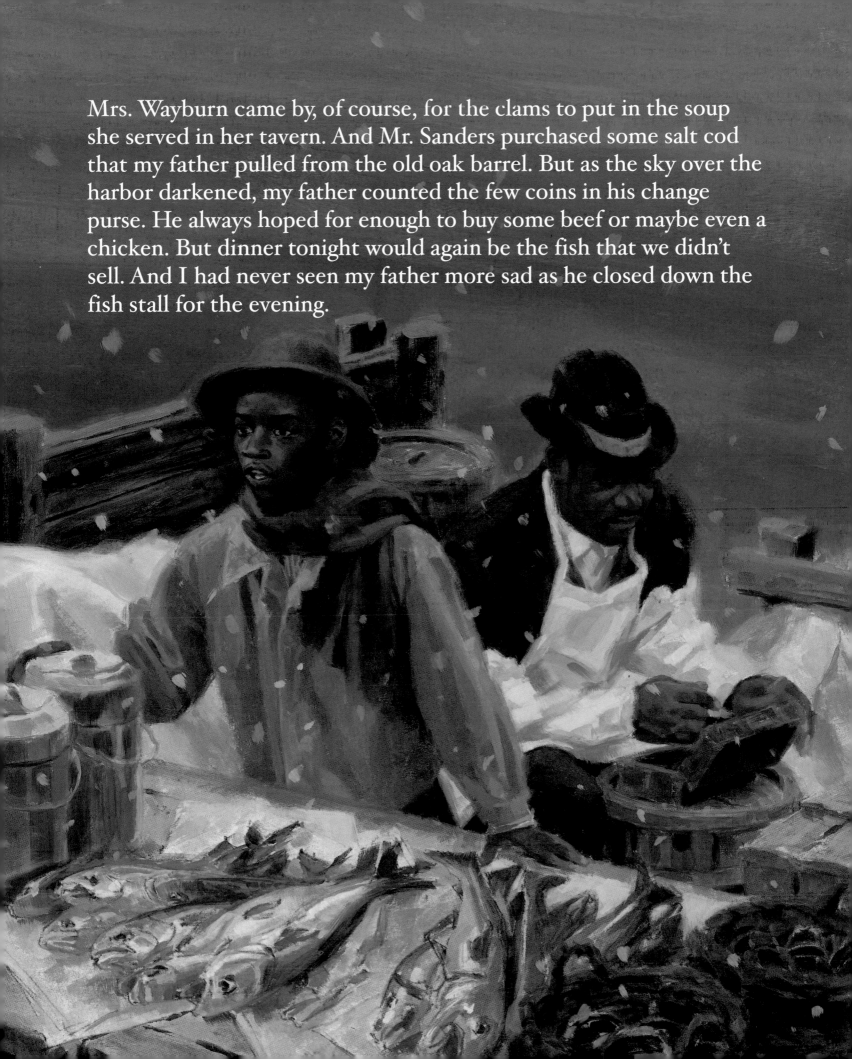

Mrs. Wayburn came by, of course, for the clams to put in the soup she served in her tavern. And Mr. Sanders purchased some salt cod that my father pulled from the old oak barrel. But as the sky over the harbor darkened, my father counted the few coins in his change purse. He always hoped for enough to buy some beef or maybe even a chicken. But dinner tonight would again be the fish that we didn't sell. And I had never seen my father more sad as he closed down the fish stall for the evening.

We walked past the other stalls run by Negro families like ours, and then moved into the wharf where the white fishmongers had their stalls. They were a little busier, but not much. We trudged the twelve blocks to our tattered row house on Woolfolk Street, the cobblestones quickly disappearing beneath the snow. Usually we talked of the stall, or of the neighbors. But this night my father spoke not a word until we stood outside the entrance to Cook's General Store. As usual, there was a group of men from our neighborhood standing beneath the awning, arguing and talking about this and that. My father said nothing, but he listened.

"Oklahoma? That's Indian Territory. You go out there, you gonna git killed. And even if you don't, ain't nobody gonna give you no farm. That's crazy." It was Rupert Johnson talking in his deep, gravelly voice. He was pointing in the face of Liberty Grosjean. Liberty could read and he often brought a newspaper to Cook's to tell what was happening in the world beyond our Baltimore row houses.

—◊—

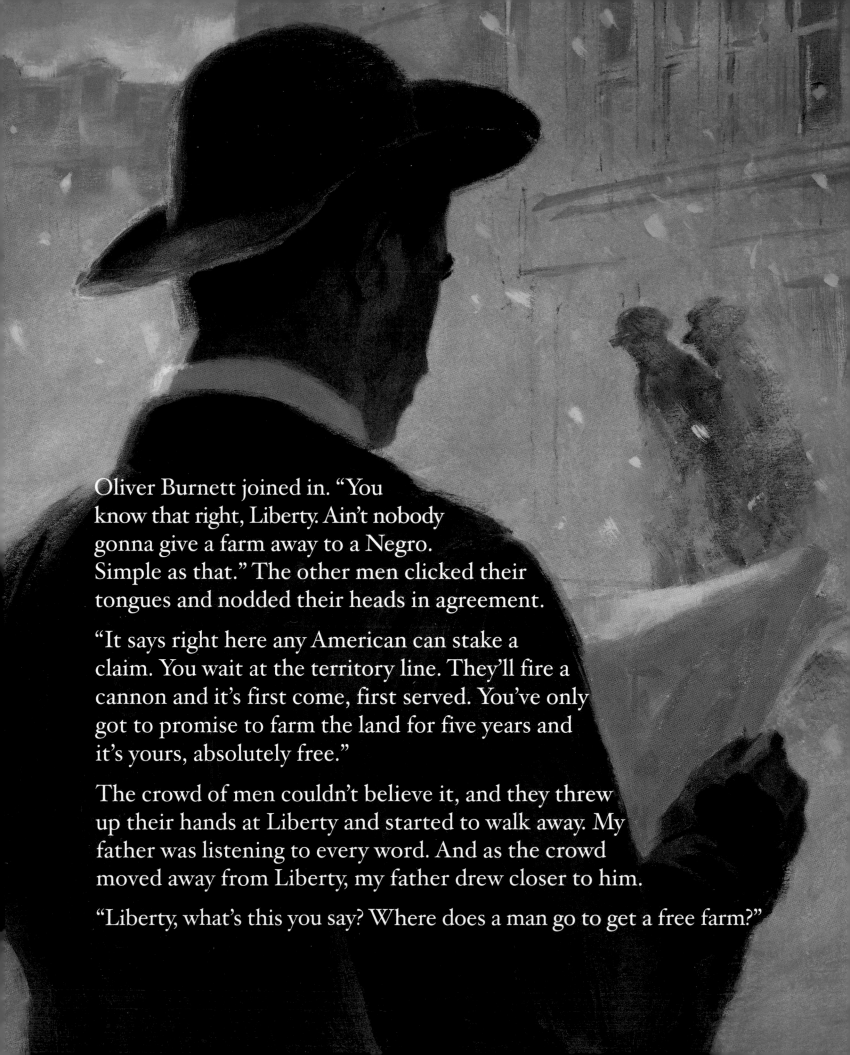

Oliver Burnett joined in. "You know that right, Liberty. Ain't nobody gonna give a farm away to a Negro. Simple as that." The other men clicked their tongues and nodded their heads in agreement.

"It says right here any American can stake a claim. You wait at the territory line. They'll fire a cannon and it's first come, first served. You've only got to promise to farm the land for five years and it's yours, absolutely free."

The crowd of men couldn't believe it, and they threw up their hands at Liberty and started to walk away. My father was listening to every word. And as the crowd moved away from Liberty, my father drew closer to him.

"Liberty, what's this you say? Where does a man go to get a free farm?"

"It's a long way, Ephraim. But this says the federal government is going to open up the Oklahoma Territory in a few weeks and let folks stake a claim. There's two million acres out there and you can have 160 of them."

"When does this happen?" my father asked.

"They're gonna fire the cannon at noon on April the 22nd," said Liberty.

"But that's just a month from now!" said my father.

"I know," said Liberty. "I'm packing tonight and I'll be on the way in just a few days."

"You're really going?" my father asked. Liberty was young, just a few years older than me. But because he had been to school and could read, he had the respect of everyone in the neighborhood.

"Ephraim," said Liberty. "Slavery is over, and we're free now. But in America a man isn't really free until he owns the land he lives on. That's true for white folks and black folks alike. A chance like this comes once in a lifetime if you're lucky."

"Moses, you run on home for supper. I'll be right behind you." I did as I was told, but I kept looking back and watching my father talking with Liberty, and I could tell my father was making plans.

—m—

I walked into the small house that was hardly big enough for our family. My mother was changing the diaper of my baby brother, Noah. My other brother, James, was playing a game with my sisters, Virginia and Lacy. Pappy and Granny, my grandfather and grandmother, were sorting through a burlap sack of small apples. I handed my mother the fish for dinner and I asked, "Momma, where's Oklahoma?"

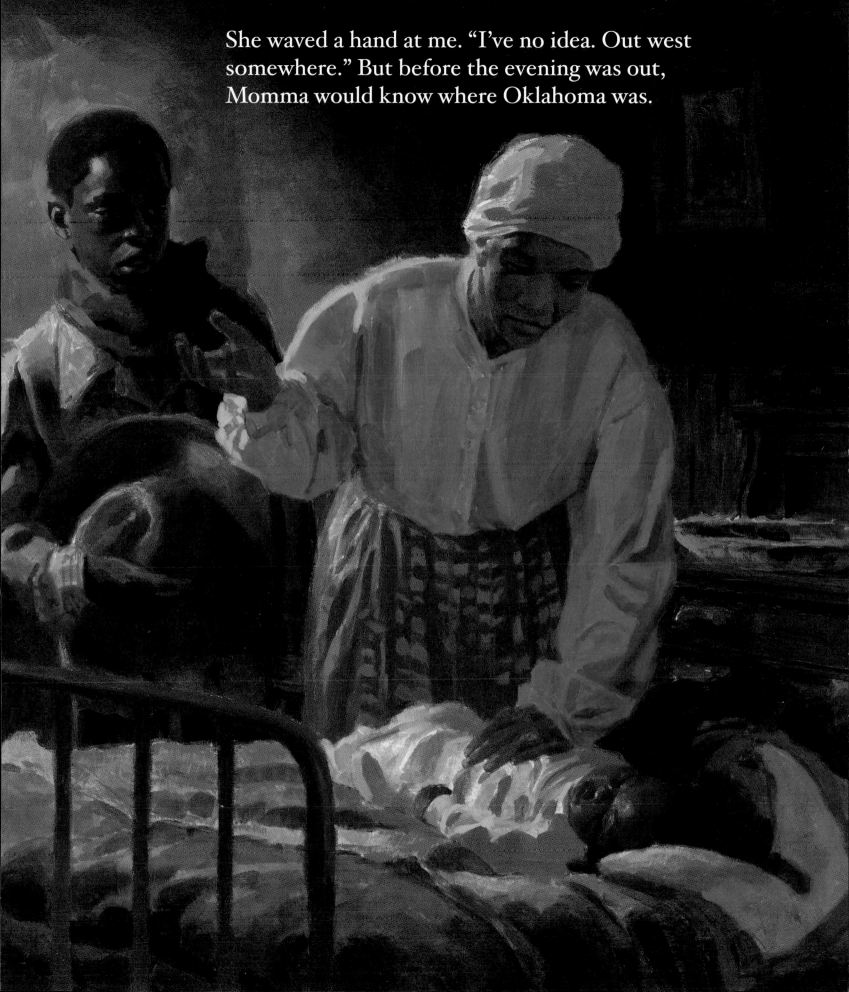

She waved a hand at me. "I've no idea. Out west somewhere." But before the evening was out, Momma would know where Oklahoma was.

As soon as my father came home he talked quietly with Pappy. I could see old Pappy's eyebrows moving up and down. Pappy grew up as a slave on a peanut farm in Virginia. He had always dreamed of farming his own land, but when slavery ended, Pappy, Granny, and my father had their freedom, but little else. They figured they might find work in a city like Baltimore, and as they learned the fish trade, the dreams of a farm drifted farther and farther away.

As my brothers and sisters and I lay in our beds, the light from the lantern glowed late into the evening and the talk between my parents and grandparents went on and on.

And the next morning my father announced that we were moving to Oklahoma.

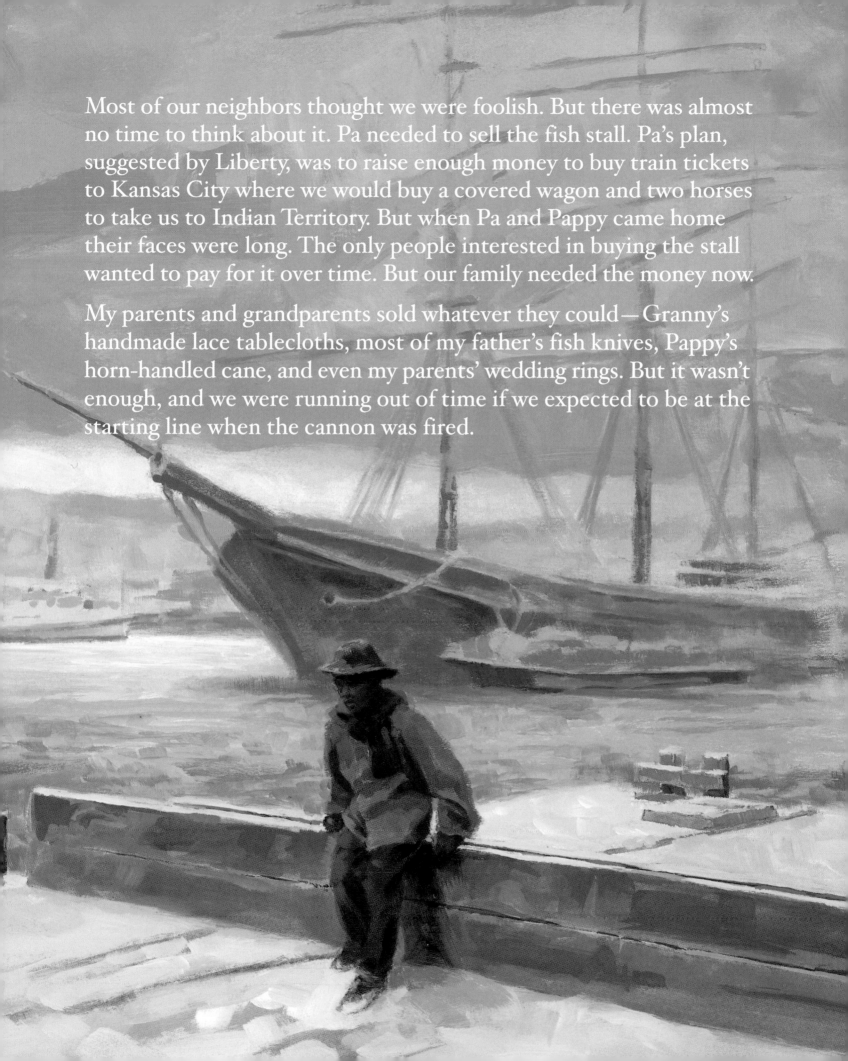

Most of our neighbors thought we were foolish. But there was almost no time to think about it. Pa needed to sell the fish stall. Pa's plan, suggested by Liberty, was to raise enough money to buy train tickets to Kansas City where we would buy a covered wagon and two horses to take us to Indian Territory. But when Pa and Pappy came home their faces were long. The only people interested in buying the stall wanted to pay for it over time. But our family needed the money now.

My parents and grandparents sold whatever they could—Granny's handmade lace tablecloths, most of my father's fish knives, Pappy's horn-handled cane, and even my parents' wedding rings. But it wasn't enough, and we were running out of time if we expected to be at the starting line when the cannon was fired.

And so it was a shock when Pa came in and rousted us from our beds and told us it was time to leave. He and Pappy had found a taker for the fish stall, a new arrival in Baltimore who had no money. But in return for the stall, he was willing to trade the one thing he did have: a wagon and two horses. And we were leaving right away!

"But Ephraim," said my mother, "how will we ever find our way? Can you find Indian Territory?"

"No," said my father. "But I know someone who can." At that moment, Liberty Grosjean appeared at the door with a huge sack on his back. In exchange for a ride to Oklahoma, Liberty would make sure we got there on time.

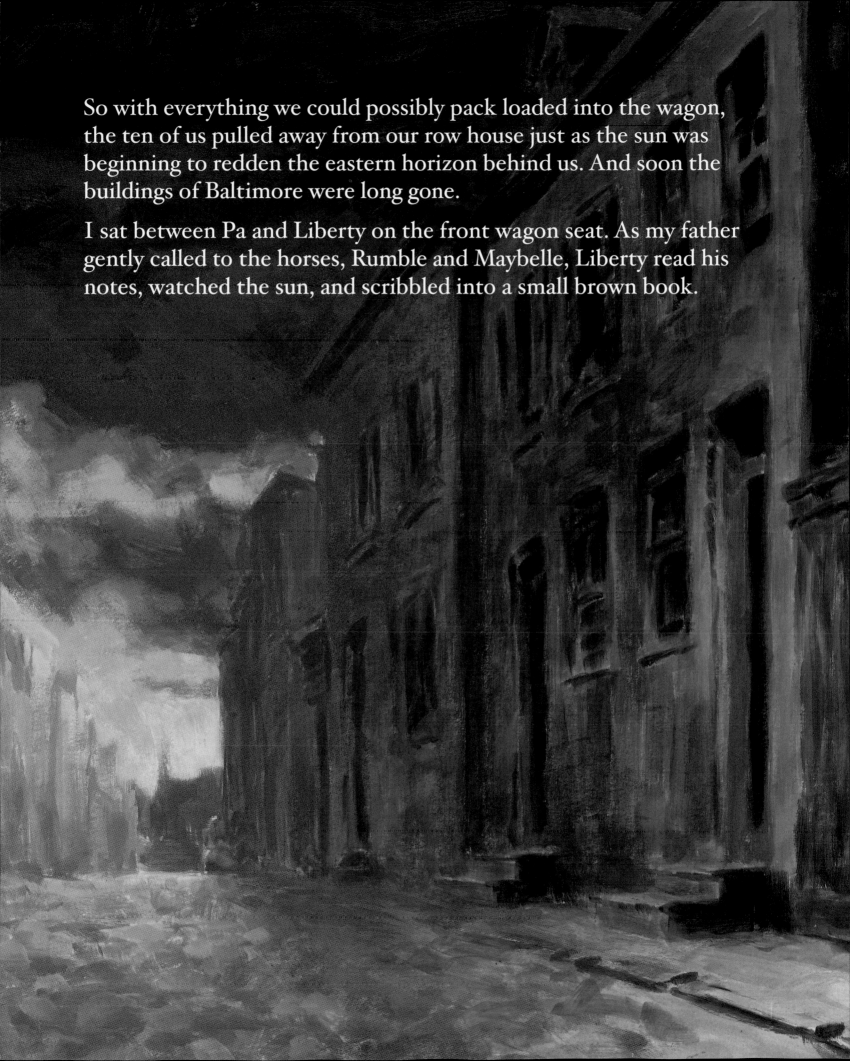

So with everything we could possibly pack loaded into the wagon, the ten of us pulled away from our row house just as the sun was beginning to redden the eastern horizon behind us. And soon the buildings of Baltimore were long gone.

I sat between Pa and Liberty on the front wagon seat. As my father gently called to the horses, Rumble and Maybelle, Liberty read his notes, watched the sun, and scribbled into a small brown book.

We rode for so many days. We rode through an ice storm in the Cumberland Mountains. It rained like I had never seen in West Virginia, and we nearly lost Maybelle in a flooded river in Kentucky. At night we made camp, often with other families making the same westward journey. We found that there were many Negro families headed for Oklahoma, people just like us who had heard that any American could stake a claim. We traded stories and supplies, songs and directions. At night Pappy would unhitch Rumble and give me a ride on his smooth back. And Liberty was teaching Pa to read by the light of the campfire.

We occasionally saw signs of trouble. A few times, white riders came trotting by telling us to go home. They said the rules had been changed and Negroes weren't allowed in the land run, but Liberty knew they were lying. One night in Tennessee, a wildcat frightened Ma half to death. We fell three days behind in Arkansas because we got lost. And most worrisome, Noah was sick with fever for nearly a week. But we knew we were getting closer and closer because the trails were getting very crowded with settlers. Liberty and Pa began to worry about whether there would be enough land for everyone.

On Saturday, April 20th, we arrived at a camp in Indian Territory near a town called Kingfisher. We had arrived just in time. We were running low on food. The trip had been hard on Maybelle and she was beginning to limp. And while little Noah was feeling better, the fever had now moved on to Pappy. He lay in the back of the wagon and told us not to worry and that he would be ready for Monday morning.

There were people and horses and wagons and mules everywhere, camped along a line of white stakes stretching across the flat Oklahoma plains. The horizon had never seemed so far away. Soldiers rode between the campfires explaining the rules for the run and warning us about straying across the boundary line too soon. And sure enough, every so often, soldiers would ride in from the boundary with a cheater under arrest.

The next night, Sunday, there were huge bonfires up and down the line of settlers. People sang songs and howled into the clear night. We made camp with lots of other Negro families. The men talked excitedly about the best way to stake a claim. Several of the men had decided that the only way to get a claim was to sneak across the line late at night.

"Look at all these folks," said one. "And there's railroad cars bringing more every couple of hours. There ain't gonna be nothing left by the time they let the Negroes in."

"Not one acre," said another. "If we don't sneak in there tonight, we might as well turn around and go home."

Lots of men nodded in agreement, but Liberty spoke up. "No. You see what's happening to the Sooners. They're being arrested and sent away. That's the best way to end up with nothing. And no one said anything about Negroes going in last. We're not Negroes here. We're Americans. We go in same as everyone else."

Several men stood to argue, but Liberty looked to my father. "Ephraim, you got any plans to turn around and go home?"

"I am home," said my father. And a silence fell on all of us as we stared into the crackling fire. I looked up and realized I had never seen a sky so full of stars. And I loved the feeling that this was our home forever.

—⌇—

Monday, April 22nd, 1889, dawned with a blazing sunshine as beautiful a spring day as there ever was. Even more settlers had arrived overnight and the crowd of homesteaders now stretched as far as I could see. No one had slept much and now there was so much excitement in the air I could barely breathe. But Ma was hollering for my Pa to come to the back of the wagon.

I followed Pa and we arrived to find my mother with her head in her hands. Pappy was not doing well. That was bad enough. But now Liberty, too, was covered in shiny sweat and shaking with fever.

My mother looked at my father. "Well," said Pa, "if we can just get to our claim..."

"Then what?" asked my mother. "Then what? We have nothing, Ephraim. There will be no house. There will be no well, no barn, no stove, no bed waiting for us. There's no doctor to call. We'll have nothing but a piece of dirt."

Granny was quietly crying, caressing Pappy's tired, weathered face. All around us, wagons and horses were moving closer to the line. I saw so many different kinds of people. They were white and black, wealthy and poor, young and old. Pa knew that Ma was right. But he did the only thing he could do.

He told us all to hang on because the ride was going to be fast and bumpy.

—◦◦◦—

For the next few hours, every settler had an eye on the sky. As the sun climbed toward high noon, Pa guided our wagon toward the line. He reached under the buckboard and handed Liberty's long rifle to me.

"It ain't loaded," he said. "But no one else has to know that."

Granny made sure Pappy and Liberty were low in the wagon and pulled James, Virginia, and Lacy close to her. Ma held Noah tightly in her arms. And we waited.

Suddenly, a canon fired from the east, a thunderous BOOM that
sent half the horses rearing back on their hind legs. But in a huge
cloud of dust, the swarm of settlers dashed into the land that looked
so golden and so precious from our camps. Those on single horses
raced way out in front and quickly disappeared on the far horizon.
The very first wagons across the line only had to travel a few hundred
yards to stake claims on the first acres up for grabs. But they were
nearly run over as they tried to stop on their new homestead with so
many others having to charge through to stake the next claim.

We had to wait a few minutes for the wagons in front of us to get on their way, but finally Rumble and Maybelle surged across the line amid the whoops and hollers of the thousands of settlers around us. The land before us finally opened up and we were dashing along with a stiff Oklahoma wind in our faces. But long gone were the smooth trails of well-traveled country. Indian Territory was covered in deep ruts and culverts and our wagon began to bounce furiously across the ditches. Liberty's head hit hard on the floor of the wagon, and James and Lacy were crying because they were so afraid.

The deep grass hid the dry creek bed ahead of us. We never saw it, and neither did Maybelle as she stumbled forward on her bad leg and lost her footing. She tumbled down and the wagon jerked violently to her side. Pa tried to pull back on Rumble's rein, but suddenly the front wheel bounced down into the culvert and as Maybelle fell, the wagon bounced hard into the air and smashed back to the ground. Pa and I flew off the buckboard and into the grass. Rumble was down, too, and both horses whinnied in pain.

While Pa made sure everyone was okay, I stared at our disaster. Our front wagon wheel was solidly lodged in the culvert. And Maybelle's reins were trapped beneath it, leaving her hopelessly jerking her head against the weight of the wagon. Pa jumped into the culvert and grabbed the forward corner of the wagon. He let out a groan and suddenly the wagon lifted just enough for Maybelle to free her rein. But Pa slipped as the weight of the wagon came crashing back down into the creek bed and right onto his left leg. The snap of my father's leg breaking filled the air just ahead of his painful scream.

Ma had to empty everyone from the wagon and it still took her, Granny and me to pull the wagon off my father. And with wagons, riders, and even runners racing by, our very dreams lay broken and beaten in a dry Oklahoma creek bed.

It was chaos. My brother and sisters were crying. My mother was dazed. Granny was trying to catch her breath, and I honestly wasn't sure Liberty was alive.

But Pappy, looking weak and haggard, let out a loud groan. He raised himself from the grass and looked out across the Oklahoma plain and turned to me.

"Moses," he said. "It's up to you."

I had no idea what he meant. But he reached into his pocket and drew out a white handkerchief.

"You take Rumble," he said. "You ride like the wind, as far and as fast as you can. And when you find our farm, you bury this handkerchief in the ground and you claim it as ours."

I expected someone to protest. But as I looked to my father, I could see that he was already trying to reach over to unharness Rumble.

Rumble was angry enough over the accident that he needed no coaxing from me to run. It was all I could do to hold on to his mane. He flew like a blur across the countryside, passing wagon and rider alike. I have no idea how long he ran or how many miles we galloped. We rode past so many stakes in the ground, so many claims that were taken, some obviously taken days ago by Sooners. But with sweat steaming off his neck and a lather foaming at his mouth, Rumble raced two other riders along a flowing creek. I knew water could mean everything for a farm, so I followed every turn and bend in the water and at last could see no stakes in the ground. I pulled Rumble to a stop and pulled from my back pocket the only possession I had. I plunged Pappy's handkerchief in the ground just as the sun was beginning to set in the western sky.

—m—

Was it mine? Was this our farm? Rumble began to drink from the creek and I sat down and wondered what to do next. I didn't even know where I was! But just before nightfall, two U.S. marshals made their way along the creek, taking stock of the claims.

"Is this your claim, son?" one of them asked me.

My voice cracked a little, but I said, "Yes, yes it is."

They looked at each other. One said, "You've got to be eighteen to make a claim, son. Are you eighteen?"

I wasn't eighteen. But what was I supposed to say? Miles away, my family lay broken and sick, counting on me. I bit my lip and looked at the marshals.

The first one smiled, raised a small notebook and asked, "What's your name, son? Nice claim you got here."

Pa was right. We were home.

It would be several days before I would be reunited with my family. A doctor had set Pa's leg and he was going to be fine. Liberty's fever had finally broken, and he was already drawing up a farm plan in his notebook. Even Maybelle was pulling through.

Sadly, Pappy would never get to see the farm he had dreamed of since his days as a slave peanut picker. But long after our house and barn had been built, and long after the first stalks of corn popped through the red soil, Pappy's handkerchief continued to wave in the ever-present Oklahoma breeze.

- The End -